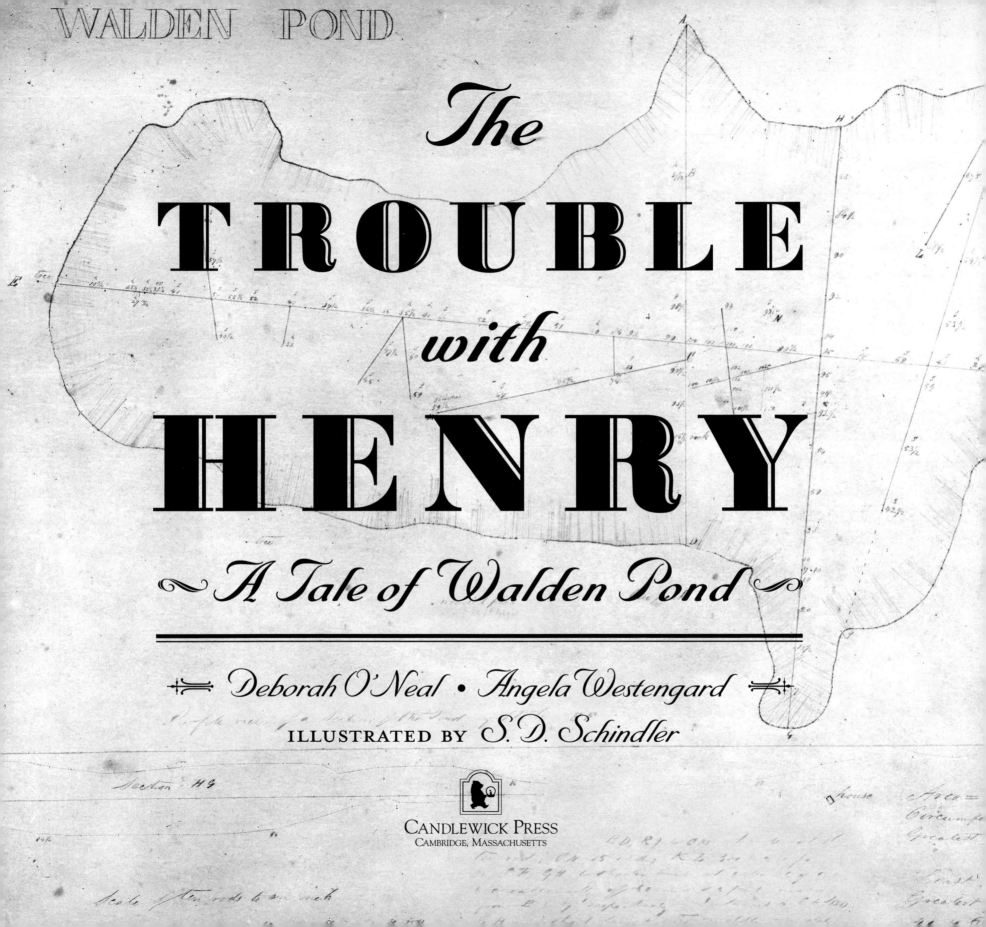

The TROUBLE with HENRY

~ A Tale of Walden Pond ~

Deborah O'Neal • Angela Westengard

ILLUSTRATED BY S. D. Schindler

CANDLEWICK PRESS
CAMBRIDGE, MASSACHUSETTS

CONCORD

Everyone in Concord knew that buying grand new things was terribly important. Everyone agreed that wearing fancy clothes and stylish hats made you a very special person. Everyone was delighted that their lovely village on the river had become a wealthy town where factories fumed and throbbed noisily day and night.

Everyone, that is, except Henry David Thoreau.

"I would rather sit on a pumpkin than a velvet couch," he told his neighbors one breezy spring morning.

"How silly!" sniffed Miss Phoebe, the town busybody, holding a frilly new parasol.

"I like my shirts soft and worn and my breeches patched at the knees," Henry said. "They feel like old friends."

"HOGWASH!" bellowed Mayor Fogg, scratching a spot under his itchy new collar.

Henry smiled. "I love to breathe the fresh morning air—not the hazy breath of smokestacks. I love to hear whippoorwills singing at noon—not machines pounding and wagons shaking the streets on their way to market."

The owner of the Concord shoe factory rubbed a gritty cinder out of his eye. "That's the trouble with you, Henry," he snorted. "You're not like the rest of us!"

The people of Concord had never been so DISGUSTED. Everyone hurried off toward the bustle and smoke of Main Street.

Everyone, that is, except Henry.

Henry had an idea. An extraordinary, some-people-might-call-it-crazy idea.

That very day, Henry hiked to Walden Pond and the nearby fringe of woods owned by his friend Mr. Emerson. The air was cool and smelled of rain and fir trees. The pond was clear and deep. Geese *carr-unkked* in the mist rising off the water.

"Here I will build myself a tiny cabin—not one inch bigger than I need," said Henry to a squirrel, who was watching him from a tall tree. "I will taste each season and listen to the voice of every creature I meet. If nature is not worth more than parasols and mills and starchy shirts, I will move back to the hubbub of Main Street and call myself the most foolish rooster in town."

Deep among the arrowy pines, where there were no rumbling wagons or belching foundries, Henry set to work. A sticky coat of pitch covered his hands and added a sharp flavor to the bread-and-butter sandwiches he ate for dinner.

Soon the days grew longer and warmer. Henry shingled the sides of his very small cabin and nailed on the roof. From his doorway, he could see the blue circle of Walden Pond and hear the shore ringing with the *trrooonnkk* of a thousand frogs.

He was so eager to live in his one-room house that he moved in before it was finished!

Everyone in Concord thought Henry was a disgrace.

Mayor Fogg called a special town meeting. He had an idea. A terrible, some-people-might-call-it-spiteful idea. "Something must be done!" he huffed.

"Most certainly," chuffed Miss Phoebe.

"Immediately!" wheezed the owner of the shoe factory, sneezing a sooty sneeze.

Even Henry's aunt Maria was nettled. "OUR NEPHEW IS CRAZY!" she shouted to Aunt Jane, who was a wee bit hard of hearing.

"THAT'S THE TROUBLE WITH HENRY. HE'S A CRAZY LITTLE ROOSTER!" Aunt Jane shouted back, even though her sister could hear perfectly well.

That very day, Mayor Fogg hitched his wagon, cracked his whip, and set out for Boston. "We'll show that Henry Thoreau how much his ridiculous pond is really worth!"

*I*n the summer months, Walden Pond wriggled and danced with ducks, fat green turtles, and tiny, spiny perch that tumbled and soared in the crystal water. The air was warm and smelled of sweet pepper bush.

Near his home in the woods, Henry planted a garden. Worms and woodchucks gobbled up more than their fair share. Still, he loved working barefoot in his field, making the earth say "beans" instead of "grass."

In autumn, when maple trees around the pond burst into fireworks of scarlet and orange and gold, Henry built himself a chimney out of old bricks. He plastered his cabin walls with mortar made of fine white sand to keep the cold out.

Inside, Henry's furniture was very humble: a bed, a desk he had made himself, two chairs for visitors, and a few crocks for cooking.

"I am the happiest man on earth," he said to a mouse sharing his warm fire and a toasty crumb.

But Henry was not happy for long.

Coming home from gathering wild apples and chestnuts one chilly afternoon, he spied Mayor Fogg and an important-looking businessman walking in the woods near Walden Pond.

They pointed at the trees and scowled. They paced off large plots of land and wrote the measurements in a book.

Henry felt scared all the way down to his ragged old boots. "What are they up to?" he wondered.

Walden Pond froze over three days before Christmas. Bubbles trapped in the ice glittered like silver coins. Sometimes deep in the night, Henry heard foxes ranging over the crust of snow. Sometimes they came right up to his windows and yelped like dogs.

As winter wore on, Henry let his whiskers grow long to warm his neck. His bean fields shriveled to a tangle of icy knots. The geese disappeared from the pond, and almost every growing thing except pines and firs shivered naked against the gray sky.

The people of Concord seemed colder, too. When Henry came into town, Miss Phoebe fumbled with her shiny new pendant and hurried away. The shoe factory owner did not bother to insult him at the post office anymore with a "Hey, Henry! Expecting a letter from a bear?" He just looked away and *UURRrrpped* from drinking the water in his rusty well.

Even Aunt Maria drew the curtains when Henry tramped up her walk.

Never had he felt so lonely. And hard as he tried, he could not shake the dreary feeling that winter would never end.

Henry went back to his cabin and waited for spring.

And he waited.

And waited.

Spring, however, dawned bleak and blustery. The streets of Concord clattered with cranky people and screaking wagons. Miss Phoebe was tired of shopping for parasols and pocketbooks and pendants—but she couldn't stop. The owner of the shoe factory was tired of rubbing his eye and sneezing and *urping*—but he couldn't stop.

On Main Street, crowds of rushing, snappish people jostled Henry without a grunt of apology. A wagon loaded with barrels splashed his coat with mud. Even the air was angry with smoke and soot.

Suddenly, Mayor Fogg called to Henry through the smoggy racket. "Have you heard the news?" he sneered, tugging at his tight new breeches. "The biggest manufacturer in Boston is going to build a TOOTHPICK FACTORY—right in the woods near your old pond! Come to the town meeting tomorrow and find out what will happen to your silly trees now."

"Toothpicks!" cried Henry. He remembered the important-looking businessman in the woods and the way he had scowled and pointed and measured. He remembered the guilty look on Miss Phoebe's face and the silence of his neighbors, dark as black ice.

"Something must be done!" Henry said.

But how could one person stop the greedy plan of a whole town?

That night, a furious wind shrieked through the pines around Henry's small home and rattled fish out of their bones in the pond. Rain lashed sideways through his garden. A sharp *CRAAACCCKKKK* of lightning struck a tall fir on the nearby hillside, splitting the tree from top to bottom with a ferocious groan. Even Henry's blazing hearth could not warm the chill inside him.

"Perhaps the trouble with me," he said to himself sadly, "is that I am a foolish little rooster after all. Tomorrow I will admit it to everyone."

But the next day dawned clear and bright at Walden Pond. Apple trees twinkled with tiny green buds. Sleepy otters crept out of their dens, and song sparrows sang *olit-olit-chip-chip-chip* across the pond.

$\mathcal{A}$t the meeting in Concord, the town hall echoed with sniffling, sneezing, huffing, chuffing, scratching, *urping*, eye-rubbing, button-popping, breeches-tugging, too-much-junk-toting people. Even the air was fussy and fretful.

"A mill near Walden Pond. How lucky we are," coughed the shoe factory owner.

"More industry means more money for us all," whimpered Miss Phoebe.

"QUIET!" cried Mayor Fogg. "Everyone in favor of turning Walden woods into a zillion toothpicks, say 'Aye'!"

An awkward hush fell over the room. Everyone looked at the floor and shuffled their feet.

Nobody was brave enough to shout, "NO! I'm sick of breathing sooty air and drinking water that tastes like rotten eggs." Nobody dared to say, "STOP! Concord has enough fancy stores and noisy factories already." And even though deep in their hearts everyone wanted to save the woods and pond, nobody uttered a sound.

Nobody, that is, except Henry.

He had an idea. A brave, some-people-might-call-it-brilliant idea.

"WAIT!" he called from the shadows in the back. Everyone turned in surprise. "I have something to show you."

$\mathcal{P}$uzzled and grumbling, the people of Concord followed Henry out through the frantic streets of town, across the meadow, and into the woods.

"HENRY IS A KNUCKLEHEAD," Aunt Jane shouted in confidence to Aunt Maria.

"A DOWNRIGHT FOOL," Aunt Maria replied.

Henry stopped at the edge of Walden Pond. The whole town crowded around him, impatient to see what was so important out there in the middle of nowhere.

But Henry did not say a word.

He didn't have to.

One by one, the grumblers and grousers noticed something strange. No wagons shook the ground. No machines throbbed noisily. No smokestacks filled the air with soot.

One by one, the people of Concord heard pewees singing in the hickory trees. They chuckled at red squirrels twitching from branch to branch. They marveled at pink mayflowers and graceful pinweeds glowing among the firs like sunshine.

One by one, the villagers dropped their parasols and pocketbooks.
They stopped their wheezing and sneezing, rubbing and scratching.
They stood perfectly still in that perfect spot, and for the first time
in years, they felt perfectly wonderful.

"This is nonsense!" shouted Mayor Fogg. He stomped back to the village, wincing in his new shoes.

Everyone else cheered and danced in the dewy emerald grass. Everyone said it would be a terrible shame to turn these lovely woods into toothpicks.

In fact, everyone thought it was high time to invite nature and simple living back to the village of Concord. Everyone—especially Henry!

"Perhaps," he thought, "I'm not such a troublesome rooster after all."

ABOUT HENRY DAVID THOREAU

He was born on July 12, 1817, in Concord, Massachusetts. There were no cars or airplanes in those days, no televisions, telephones, computers, faxes, or e-mail. Machines had just begun to produce goods like cloth, dishes, furniture, and even toys, which had always been made by hand.

Henry was worried because natural resources were destroyed as mills and factories polluted the air and rivers. He wrote several books and essays—including "Walking," *The Maine Woods,* and the classic *Walden*—asking people to protect the earth and care for each other. After all, Henry once said, "Heaven is under our feet as well as over our heads."

He also had strong beliefs about right and wrong. Long before it was popular, Henry wrote about the ancient wisdom of Native Americans and their respect for nature. He helped runaway slaves escape to Canada on the Underground Railroad. His life and writings have influenced many great people, including Mohandas Gandhi and Martin Luther King Jr.

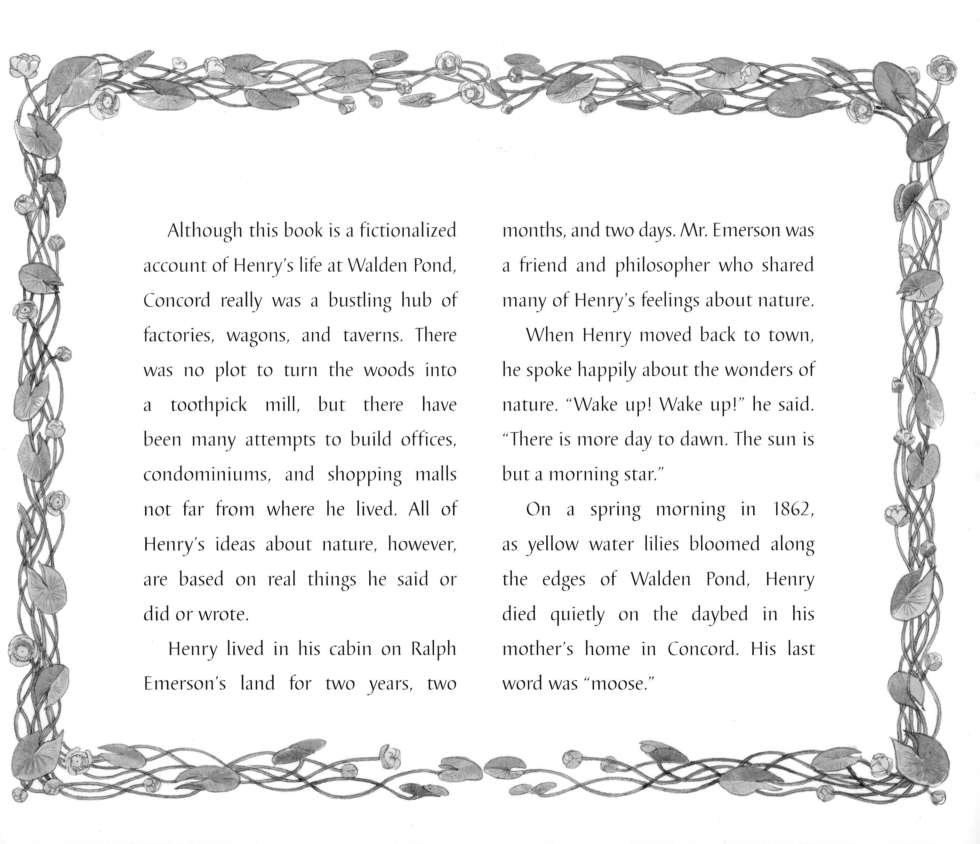

Although this book is a fictionalized account of Henry's life at Walden Pond, Concord really was a bustling hub of factories, wagons, and taverns. There was no plot to turn the woods into a toothpick mill, but there have been many attempts to build offices, condominiums, and shopping malls not far from where he lived. All of Henry's ideas about nature, however, are based on real things he said or did or wrote.

Henry lived in his cabin on Ralph Emerson's land for two years, two months, and two days. Mr. Emerson was a friend and philosopher who shared many of Henry's feelings about nature.

When Henry moved back to town, he spoke happily about the wonders of nature. "Wake up! Wake up!" he said. "There is more day to dawn. The sun is but a morning star."

On a spring morning in 1862, as yellow water lilies bloomed along the edges of Walden Pond, Henry died quietly on the daybed in his mother's home in Concord. His last word was "moose."

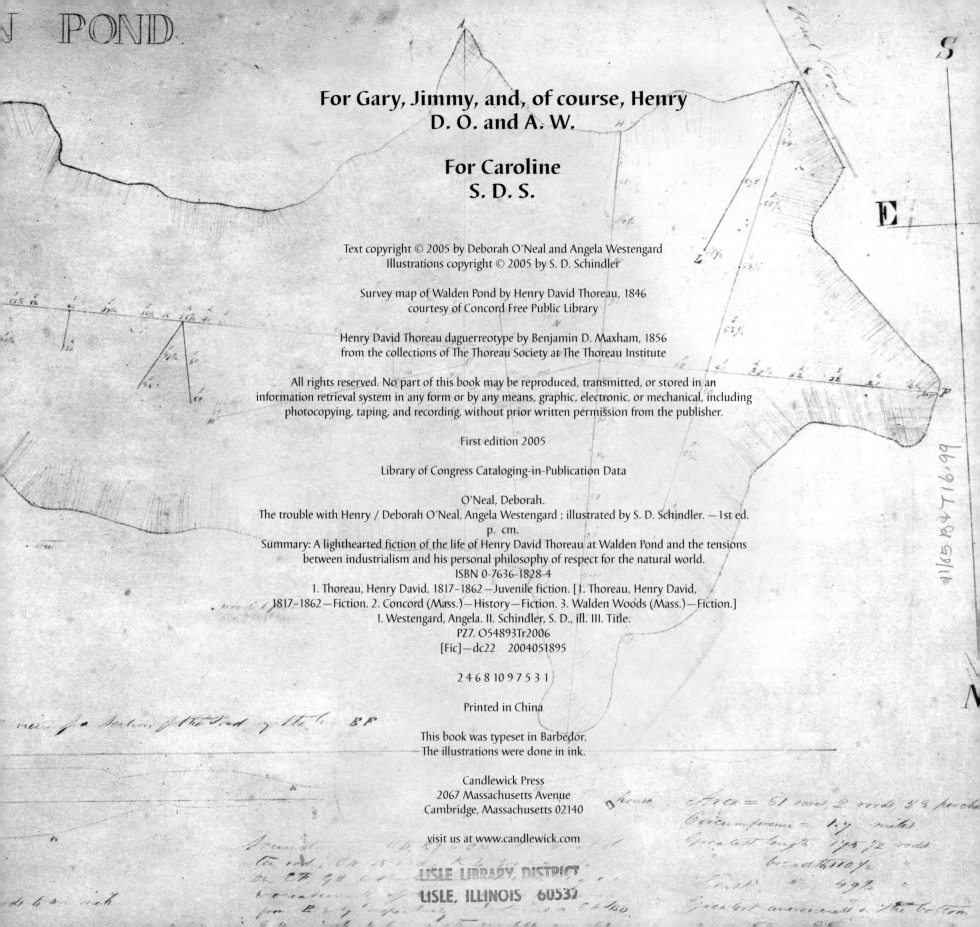

For Gary, Jimmy, and, of course, Henry
D. O. and A. W.

For Caroline
S. D. S.

Text copyright © 2005 by Deborah O'Neal and Angela Westengard
Illustrations copyright © 2005 by S. D. Schindler

Survey map of Walden Pond by Henry David Thoreau, 1846
courtesy of Concord Free Public Library

Henry David Thoreau daguerreotype by Benjamin D. Maxham, 1856
from the collections of The Thoreau Society at The Thoreau Institute

First edition 2005

Library of Congress Cataloging-in-Publication Data

O'Neal, Deborah.
The trouble with Henry / Deborah O'Neal, Angela Westengard ; illustrated by S. D. Schindler. —1st ed.
p. cm.
Summary: A lighthearted fiction of the life of Henry David Thoreau at Walden Pond and the tensions between industrialism and his personal philosophy of respect for the natural world.
ISBN 0-7636-1828-4
1. Thoreau, Henry David, 1817–1862—Juvenile fiction. [1. Thoreau, Henry David, 1817–1862—Fiction. 2. Concord (Mass.)—History—Fiction. 3. Walden Woods (Mass.)—Fiction.]
I. Westengard, Angela. II. Schindler, S. D., ill. III. Title.
PZ7. O54893Tr2006
[Fic]—dc22   2004051895

2 4 6 8 10 9 7 5 3 1

Printed in China

This book was typeset in Barbedor.
The illustrations were done in ink.

Candlewick Press
2067 Massachusetts Avenue
Cambridge, Massachusetts 02140

visit us at www.candlewick.com